THIS CANDLEWICK BOOK BELONGS TO:

_____

_____

_____

_____

To Joe
S. M.

For Rachel
I. B.

ISBN 0-590-28285-9

Text copyright © 1996 by Sam McBratney.
Illustrations copyright © 1996 by Ivan Bates. All rights reserved. Published by
Scholastic Inc., 555 Broadway, New York, NY 10012, by arrangement with
Candlewick Press. SCHOLASTIC and associated logos are trademarks and/or registered
trademarks of Scholastic Inc.

12 11 10 9 8 7 6 5 4 3 2 1   8 9/9 0 1 2 3/0

Printed in the U.S.A.   23

First Scholastic printing, January 1998

JUST ONE!

Sam McBratney

illustrated by Ivan Bates

SCHOLASTIC INC.

New York   Toronto   London   Auckland   Sydney

Down in the woods, little Digger was
picking blackberries with the old gray
squirrel who looked after him.
They picked blackberries along by the
river, and they picked them
in the shady lane.
Soon they had
a big pile of
blackberries.

"Is this the biggest pile of blackberries
you've ever seen?" said little Digger to
Old-and-Gray.
"Yes it is," replied Old-and-Gray.
"I'll go and look for something to
put them in, or we'll never carry
them home."
"Will I be in charge of our blackberries
while you're away?" asked Digger.
"Yes. But don't eat too many—
just a few," said Old-and-Gray.
And off he went to find something
to put the blackberries in.

A country mouse ran out of the cornfield at the edge of the woods. She sat down beside Digger and the pile of blackberries. "I'm in charge of all these," said Digger. "They look yummy," said the mouse. "Do you think I could have some?" "Well, don't eat too many," said Digger. "Just a few."

The country mouse ate some of the blackberries, and so did little Digger.

A flatfooted duck waddled up from the river. He looked at Digger, and the country mouse, and then he pointed his beak at the pile of blackberries. "Very nice indeed," said the duck. "I'm in charge of them," said Digger. "Do you think I could have some?" asked the duck. "Well, not too many," said Digger. "Just a few."

The flatfooted duck ate some of the blackberries, and so did Digger and the country mouse.

Then a bouncy baby rabbit came out of the woods. She hopped right around the blackberries and sat down beside Digger, and the duck, and the country mouse. "Do you think I could taste some of those yummy blackberries?" she said. "Well, not too many," said Digger. "You can just have a few."

The bouncy baby rabbit ate some of the blackberries, and so did Digger and the duck and the country mouse.

Then they heard the noise of someone approaching through the woods. Old-and-Gray was coming back with something to hold the blackberries.

"I hope there won't be too many to carry in this," he said as he came closer.
"No," said Digger, looking at the pile of blackberries. "Not too many . . .

just one!"